GREETINGS FROM
ANCIENT
GREECE

by Joanne Basham

illustrated by Jack Crane

Harcourt

Orlando   Boston   Dallas   Chicago   San Diego

Visit *The Learning Site!*

www.harcourtschool.com

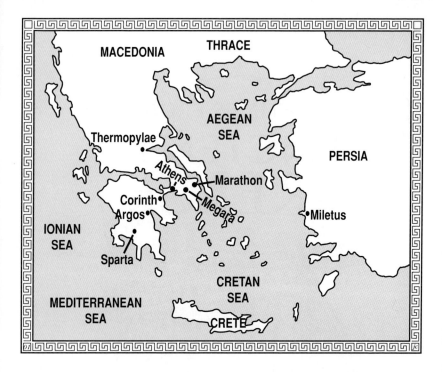

Ancient Greece was divided into different regions, each one controlled by a *polis*, or city-state. Each city-state had its own customs and educational system.

The Greeks were fiercely proud of their city-states; each Greek citizen thought his or her city-state was the finest.

This book contains journal entries of two fictional boys from ancient Greece; one boy comes from Athens, the other from Sparta. As you read their journal entries, you will begin to see some of the cultural, educational, and philosophical differences between the city-states of Athens and Sparta. Think about which of these two city-states you would have preferred to live in if you had been born in ancient Greece.

Arcos, an Athenian boy, writes:

My lyre lesson was less than successful today. Perhaps that is because my teacher does not like me—at least that is how it seems. I love music, and I am willing to work hard. Unfortunately, my teacher does not like it when I compose my own little pieces. He calls it laziness. Imagine!

Today we had a pleasant visit from Onerus, my cousin. She stopped by to tell us of her impending marriage to a man from Corinth. My parents are delighted for her. Corinth is a prosperous port city. Perhaps this will open up new opportunities for our families.

Tarnus, a young Spartan, writes:

Again I have failed a test! The war drills are difficult and ask the most that one can deliver. The punishment for being imperfect is harsh. Even worse, though, is the embarrassment when the older boys jeer afterward. This is how great Sparta teaches its boys to be fearless warriors. I must learn to put up with such discomfort without bellowing. I miss my home.

Arcos, an Athenian boy, writes:

I have just returned from a hike in the countryside with my friend, Cyrus. The sun's heat was fierce, but the olive groves gave welcome shade while we ate lunch.

Cyrus has great skill at reciting Homer's poetry! Even the teachers are impressed. With his keen memory and ability to speak publicly, perhaps he will become a great Athenian statesman some day.

My friend the future statesman lost our race home though! Who knows? Perhaps I will train to become an Olympic athlete. That would bring honor to my polis of Athens!

Tarnus, a young Spartan, writes:

Success! Today our team won a mock battle. We planned our strategy carefully. Our moves were flawless, if I do say so myself. Triumphant shouts broke out when we won, and there were a lot of friendly thumps on the back.

We entered the barracks, our home, and headed for the dining hall. Usually our meals are skimpy and tasteless. This meal was delicious! Perhaps this was a reward for our performance today. The platters on the table held freshly baked bread, goat cheese—even figs! This was not the usual moldy stuff disguised as food. For the first time in ages, I did not feel hungry after a meal.

I am slowly getting used to life in the barracks. I had better get used to it, since I probably will live here until I am 60 years old! It is the same for all Spartan boys, except those who are not citizens.

One of the boys is fairly friendly. He saved me from a few skirmishes with those brutes, the older boys. His name is Nikos, and he seems to be a good choice for a friend. He may be able to help me become more brave and cunning. These skills are extremely important to a future warrior of Sparta! I will continue working to improve my skills so that one day I will make the leaders of Sparta proud to have such a fine warrior as Tarnus in their ranks!

Arcos writes:

Today is my twelfth birthday. Mother instructed the slaves to prepare a special feast in my honor. Even my sisters helped. Father was also home for the celebration.

Since the weather was so fair, we ate in the courtyard. The slaves seemed proud of their efforts. Good cooking is just one of our slaves' many virtues. Father and Mother treat them well. In return, the slaves are loyal to us.

After our delicious dinner, we listened as Father retold the story of his humorous first attempts at wrestling when he was just a small boy. He winked at me as he talked. I think he is proud of my skill at wrestling so far. That pleases me.

I enjoyed being together with my family in the courtyard. It is not every day that we all meet for a meal. I am away at school all day. Father's work takes him away for days at a time, sometimes much longer. Mother and the girls rarely go out, except for special occasions or to visit a nearby relative.

Speaking of Mother, she wove the most beautiful new tunic for my birthday. Since it is warm now, it is woven of linen instead of the wool we wear in the cold months. Mother is a very talented weaver!

The girls gave me a fine new hairbrush. A jeweled ring was Father's gift. He must have bought it while he was away. I am grateful for my gifts. I should get some sleep now. School starts early!

Tarnus writes:

I am so glad that Nikos is my friend. Now I am 12; a full four years have passed since I came to the barracks, and only now do I have a true friend. We manage to find something to laugh about every day, making this hard life less unbearable.

For the past few days, we have been marching without shoes. This is an important part of our training to be soldiers. No one complains. There is no point. There is something to be said for our stark and harsh life, though. Our group is beginning to work very well together. Hardship sometimes makes people work as a team, I think. We are becoming proud of our abilities, and we are proud to be Spartans.

I know that some people think our ways are harsh. Much of our education involves rigorous exercise and overcoming physical challenges. Girls as well as boys need to be educated to stay strong. From what I hear, Sparta's women are not only the strongest but also the freest, compared with women in other city-states. In Sparta women can speak openly among men, and if you encounter wrestlers or racers, they might very well be women!

Here, as everywhere in Greece, however, women are not citizens. Sparta is ruled by aristocrats, and only male aristocrats can be citizens. We also have many slaves and middle-class people. The lives of slaves and middle-class people are not so bad. Many of our police are slaves! Slaves live much like poor people, working in the fields, in shops, and on ships. I have heard that there are more slaves in Sparta than there are citizens!

I must get to sleep. Yesterday one of the other boys had to rouse me out of a deep sleep at dawn. Sleeping late is frowned upon, let me tell you.

Arcos writes:

Father is away on government business again. There is talk of trouble with Sparta. I am nervous. The very thought of a war with those ruthless warriors is enough to worry any intelligent person—not that proud Athens should be worried. We have our own soldiers, all fiercely ready to protect our democratic system. Every citizen votes, and every citizen defends his city-state in time of need. I think Athenians, being better educated, will triumph over the Spartans.

At school our teacher has been telling us about the wars with Persia. They happened not that long ago, he said, so we should pay close attention.

Those wars began because the Persian city state of Miletus wanted to leave the Persian Empire. Miletus wanted to join the Greek colonial empire. The Persian emperor, Darius, did not approve of this plan, so he challenged the Greek navy. He lost. Our navy was great and still is! After that, Darius declared war on Athens and its allies.

Darius and his forces captured several city states along the Macedonian coast, but his luck ran out. As his forces continued toward Athens, a terrific storm drowned his fleet of ships.

Darius must have been a very stubborn man. One year later he asked for all the Greek city-states to bow down to him and pay him money. He should have known that freedom-loving Greeks would never agree! There was a great battle at Marathon. The Greeks used some wonderful military strategies—light infantry, or foot soldiers, and a military formation known as a phalanx.

We beat the Persians decisively. They lost about 6,400 men. We lost only 192.

Then, our teacher said, the Persians planned to attack Athens again. A famous runner, Pheidippides, was sent to warn Athens. He made the run, and Athens had time to prepare for the battle at Marathon, northeast of Athens. Poor Pheidippides died after his twenty-mile run. His bravery and endurance were so appreciated that the Greeks have included a marathon run at all future Olympic Games.

Well, I must get back to my studies. I would be proud to fight for my country the way that generation of Greeks did.

Tarnus writes:

We have drilled all day with spears and bows and arrows. Every muscle aches, but I don't even mind. It feels wonderful to have done my best. I am beginning to believe that I have what it takes to become a great soldier and athlete. Pain and struggle are part of my life, and I have risen above them. Nikos and I keep trying to outdo each other and everyone else. Competition is enjoyable, although I have not yet learned to be a gracious loser!

Nikos and I have added another skill to our list. We have learned how to steal food. If we are caught, we will be beaten severely. So far we have made a few successful attempts—a bit of salted fish here, a loaf of bread there. My mother would not approve of this dishonesty, and she would be right. It is a shame to have to steal food, but when one is so very hungry, it is tempting.

Some boys in the barracks say that the Athenians are becoming a problem and that there may be some military action in the future. If I am of an age to be a soldier when this occurs, I will be happy to protect the honor of Sparta. I am a little afraid, though. So far our life has been one of preparation. Now it seems that there may be very real dangers in our future.

Arcos writes:

Cyrus and I went on a fishing trip for a few days with Cyrus's father. I loved sailing and the freedom of being on the sea. Fishing was more difficult than I had thought, but the sailors realized that we were new at this and helped with the heavy, unwieldy nets. We had an amazing catch!

Supper consisted of grilled fish with lemon and thyme, served with bread and olive oil. It tasted like no other fish supper I had ever had. We landed, unloaded the fish, and returned home sunburned, tired, and laughing.

Today it was back to school. Our teacher continued telling us about the Persian Wars. We learned that Xerxes, the son of Darius, also tried to defeat the Greeks. I suppose he wanted to do this to please his father. Under Xerxes one army marched to Thermopylae, a tiny mountain pass defended by an impressive army of Spartans.

The Spartans were forceful, but after a few days, some of Xerxes' special troops found another entrance to the pass and wiped out the Spartans.

I have to admit, hearing this made me sympathetic toward the Spartan army, as different as we are. The Persians gave them such a cruel and crushing blow. I will remember Thermopylae.

Of course, the Greeks won in the end, as they always will. Perhaps that is what Sparta, Athens, Corinth, and the other city-states have to learn—we are all Greeks.

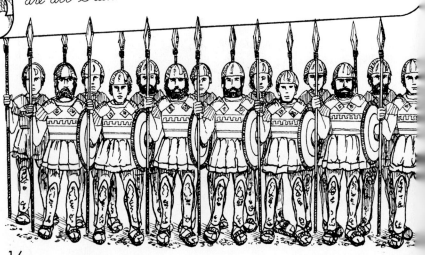